squid. That's a funny word. squid.

My new X ray goggles allow me to see bones.

Chilly, I hope you know your machines are never going to work. Everybody knows it but you. JUST GIVE UP.

-Vinnie

Vinnie

p.s. I threw your lunchbox in the deep waters. ha ha ha ha ha ha ha

For Isaac: always think beyond your iceberg.
My goal is to make you proud of me.—J.R.

Text and illustrations copyright © 2018 by Jarrett Rutland.
First published in the United States, Great Britain, Canada, Australia, and New Zealand in 2018
by NorthSouth Books, Inc., an imprint of NordSüd Verlag AG, CH-8050 Zürich, Switzerland.

Distributed in the United States by NorthSouth Books, Inc., New York 10016.
Library of Congress Cataloging-in-Publication Data is available.
ISBN: 978-0-7358-4283-0
Printed in Latvia by Livonia Print, Riga, 2018.
1 3 5 7 9 · 10 8 6 4 2
www.northsouth.com

CHILLY DA VINCI

J. RUTLAND

North
South

My name is Chilly, and while others do "penguin" things, I build machines.

Unfortunately, they don't always work.

I told you so!

After the Big Crack Setback, a large orca has found us, like crumbs on a floating plate. It is taking bites out of the iceberg. I swear I heard it giggle.

The others agreed when Vinnie said I was "not good at being a penguin." They'll change their minds when my new machine gets us back to Vinci.

First, I'll draw up my plans.... I'll use sea junk, and build the *Polar Roller,* which will skim across the water in style!

metal panels (20)

It sank like a stone! What was I thinking?
One cannot simply drive across the water.
My brain is full of seawater, and my
sketchbook is full of goof-ups.

Did I mention it wouldn't move anyway
if it had to drag Mr. Plumpy Fin? Luckily
all the penguins made it out safely.

The orca didn't give up either.

NOTE: I am terrible at thinking. I should do it less. How can I, a tiny gathering of flightless feathers, move an iceberg? My pulleys didn't pulley. My engine didn't engine.

Boy, Plumpy Fin really likes splashes. If I were to look at the bite—I mean the bright—side, I have been in the air a lot longer than on the *Good Bird*.

Mr. Plumpy Fin has eaten most of the iceberg. We're running out of time. I wish I was a seagull, just using the wind to drift around and look at stars. . . . Wait! *Wind!*

NOTE: wind. The gulls use only enough
effort to let the wind carry them.

Nature does most of the work.

whoosh.

The air current was...

Gale made the waves...

Could they blow my machine?

I've got it! I'll revisit something that did not work before: a flying machine.

I'll use leather for the wings so they won't tear. And I'll use bones. They're light but still strong. If it works, it will carry everyone home to Vinci.

I've logged a ton of drawings of seagull wings acting as sails.

A little rope there, a pulley here, and ... the *Great Bird* is ready!

It's a relief I'm not dropping like a glacier rock. I wonder if I could spit on Plumpy Fin from here.

The penguins are chanting my name!

I used air currents to ease down onto the berg, like a snowflake. The penguins will hug me and tell me they believed in me.

skkrrrr

No time for hugs! The iceberg is
shrinking, and Plumpy Fin is circling.

I only let Vinnie come because he brought fritters.

The landing went fine.
A little snow up the beak
never hurt anyone.

WHOOSH!!

We made it at last!
As soon as we stopped,
penguins rushed to greet us.

barnacle.

bar-nackle.

swaddle swaddle

bee bop bee

poop